AW, NUTS!

Written and illustrated by Rob McClurkan

HARPER
An Imprint of HarperCollinsPublishers

Bethany
Cassidy
Houston

For information address HarperCollins Children's Books, a division of HarperCollins Publishers, 195 Broadway, New York, NY 10007.   www.harpercollinschildrens.com   Library of Congress Cataloging-in-Publication Data   McClurkan, Rob, author, illustrator.   Aw, nuts! / written and Illustrated by Rob McClurkan. — First edition.   pages cm   Summary: When Squirrel goes after the perfect acorn, on foot, in a taxi, and even by pogo stick, one thing after another goes wrong.   ISBN 978-0-06-231729-2 (hardcover : alk. paper)   [1. Squirrels—Fiction. 2. Acorns—Fiction. 3. Tall tales.] 1. Title.   PZ7.M47841419473Aw 2014   [E]—dc23   2013037295   CIP   AC   The artist used Photoshop to create the digital illustrations for this book.   Typography by Rachel Zegar   14 15 16 17 18 SCP 10 9 8 7 6 5 4 3 2 1 ❖ First Edition

Squirrel LOVED acorns.

He would roast them. He would toast them.
He would grill them. He would chill them.

Every fall, Squirrel would collect acorns.
One day, he saw the most delicious-looking
acorn he had ever seen. He had to have it.

He pushed . . .

he shoved . . .

until it finally fit.
But then . . .

Poor Squirrel! All his acorns were gone!
Then he heard it.

HEY,
COME BACK
HERE!

It was his prized acorn, bouncing down the street.

"Boing
Boing
Boing"

Grabbing his sneakers, Squirrel ran after the acorn as fast as he could.

Until he lost a shoe.

So Squirrel jumped into a taxi,

but the taxi ran out of gas.

Luckily, on the same corner was a pogo stick.

Not as lucky, Squirrel bounced right into a manhole.

A truck was passing by. So Squirrel grabbed hold of it.

Who's he calling a nut?

But the truck brought him all the way to Bucksnort, Tennessee.

From there . . .

He rode a dog that chased its tail.

He hopped into a boat that sprang a leak.

He jumped on a horse that threw him off.

He hitched a ride on
a little girl's bike.

Then he ended up
at a birthday party.

I love
you!

Hug
attack!

AW,
NUTS!

My
turn!

That's when he caught hold of a big red balloon.
The balloon carried him high into the air, where . . .

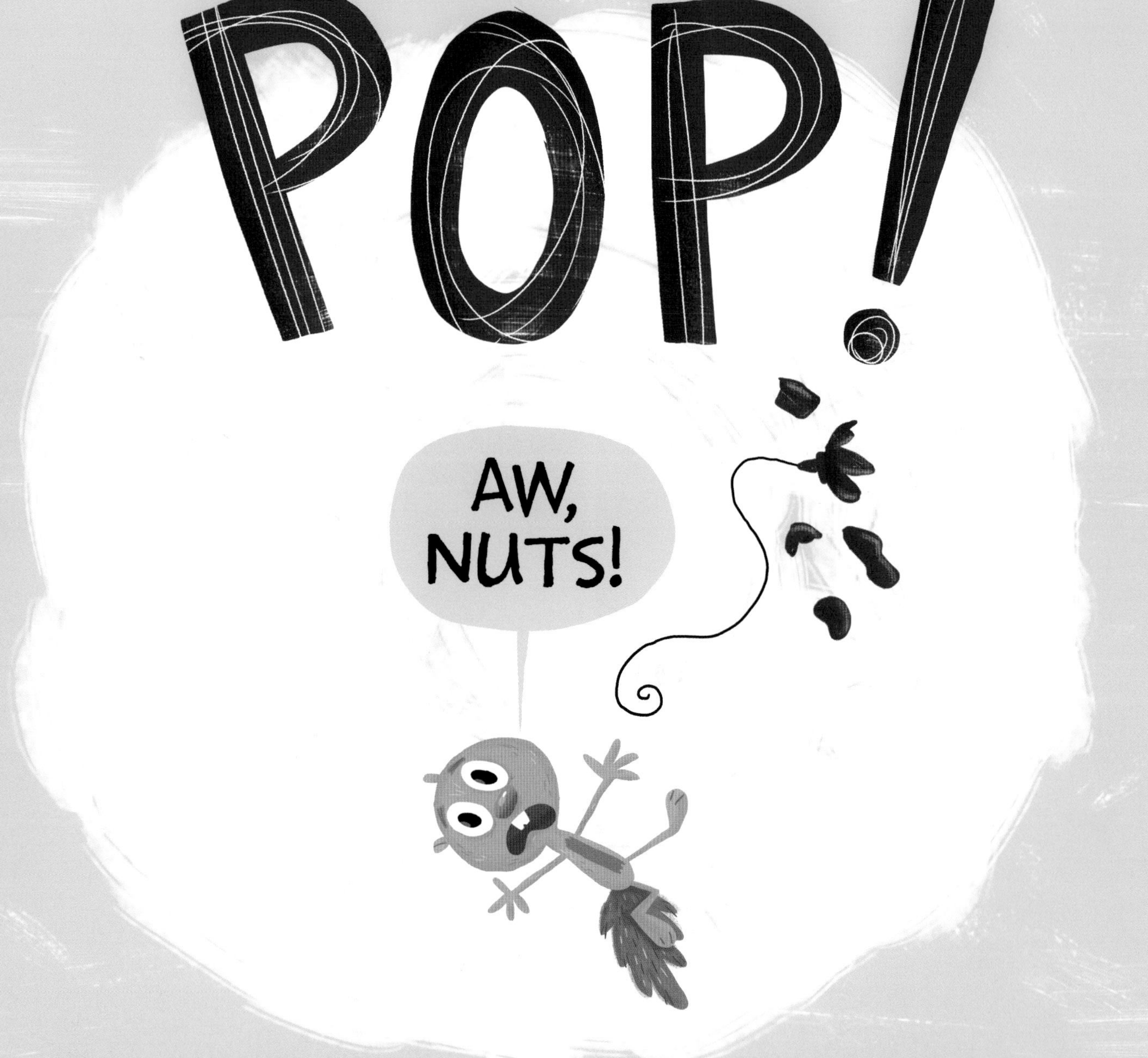
POP!
AW, NUTS!

SPLAT!

At that exact moment the acorn rolled to a stop.

Back home, Squirrel was finally about to dig into the most delicious-looking acorn ever. Then, all of a sudden, a new most delicious-looking acorn dropped from the sky.

Aw, nuts!